Lose That Tooth!

MRS. ROBINSON'S CLASS

by Peter Maloney
and Felicia Zekauskas

SCHOLASTIC INC.

New York   Toronto   London   Auckland   Sydney
Mexico City   New Delhi   Hong Kong   Buenos Aires

For Alex and Benjamin

ISBN 0-439-67639-8

12 11 10 9 8 7 6 5 4 3   6 7 8 9 10/0

Printed in the U.S.A.
First printing, April 2005

CHAPTER 1
Say "Cheese!"

"Don't forget," said Mrs. Robinson, "we're having our class picture taken on Friday!"

"And what are we going to do when the photographer tells us to say 'Cheese'?"

Everyone in the class smiled.

Except Peter.

"What's wrong?" Felicia asked Peter.

"I'm not going to smile for the class picture," said Peter.

"Why not?" asked Felicia.

"Because *everybody* is missing a tooth," said Peter.

"Except me!"

"But you have a great smile," said
Felicia. "Even with all your teeth."

CHAPTER 2

The Tooth Unfairy

The next day, Russ Deluca came to school smiling.

"I lost another tooth," said Russ. "And look what the tooth fairy left me!" Russ waved a dollar bill in the air.

"I've already made three dollars off these teeth," said Russ. "And I plan to make a lot more!"

Peter felt worse than ever.
Some of his classmates had lost
several teeth.
All Peter had was one front tooth that
barely jiggled.
"It's just not fair," he said.

CHAPTER 3
Yank That Tooth

After school, Peter's mom took him to the dentist for a checkup.

"Your teeth are in great shape," said Dr. Ragen.

Peter frowned.

"What's wrong?" asked Dr. Ragen.

"All my classmates are losing their teeth," said Peter. "And I need to lose one, too — by Friday."

"Well, one of your front teeth is a little bit loose," said Dr. Ragen.

"Maybe you could pull it out for me," said Peter.

Dr. Ragen laughed.
"Children's teeth are like leaves," he said. "They fall out when they're ready."

CHAPTER 4

An Unexpected Trip

The next morning, Peter's mom
dressed him for the class photo.

"You look nice all dressed up," said
Felicia.
Peter blushed.
But he still didn't smile.

"I was thinking about your tooth problem," said Felicia.
She pulled out a pack of Black Coal chewing gum.
"Maybe we could make it look like you lost a tooth," she said.

Felicia quickly chewed a stick of gum
and covered a front tooth with it.
Peter shook his head.
"I can't do it," he said. "Mrs. Robinson
says no gum in school."

Suddenly, Peter went crashing to the
sidewalk.
Someone had tripped him!

Someone wearing green sneakers!
Someone who was now laughing
behind a tree.
"That's not funny, Russ Deluca!" said
Felicia.

CHAPTER 5
Something's Missing!

Peter covered his mouth with his hand.
"Are you alright?" asked Felicia.

"I think so," mumbled Peter.

Then Peter took his hand away.
Felicia gasped!

"Your front tooth is missing!" she
cried.

"No, it's not," said Peter.
He held out his hand.
"It's right here."

CHAPTER 6
Say "Cheese," Again!

MRS. ROBINSON'S CLASS

Mrs. Robinson lined up the children for the class picture.

The photographer told everybody to say "Cheese!"

Everybody smiled.
Especially Peter.